MOS

LEAFLETTE

PIPPY

OAKUM

The BeWILDerbats

By Tom Blofeld

Illustrated By Steve Pearce

Holly Day & Bump Publishing

First published in Great Britain by Holly Day and Bump Publishing.

ISBN 978-0-95555-432-2

10 9 8 7 6 5 4 3 2 1

www.BeWILDerwood.co.uk

Produced by Navigator Guides www.navigatorguides.com
Printed in the UK on behalf of JFDI Print Services Ltd

To Simon and Maggie
with all my love

CONTENTS

The Bust Nuts

It was a leafy sort of autumn day in Bewilderwood and the clouds were really trying not to get in the way of the sun. Yesterday, everyone in the Twiggle village had done all of their washing in the warm wind, so today the villagers were gathered on the main platform, high up in the trees, having a chat. Twiggles always build their villages among the branches of trees.

The Twiggles were deciding what to do with such a nice day.

"We could go for a nut-hunt," suggested a wiry old Twiggle. "I haven't had nutbug crunch for ages."

This seemed to everybody to be a very sensible idea and they were just getting their baskets when Moss had a clever thought. Moss was a Marsh Boggle who had married a pretty Twiggle named Leaflette and had come to live in the Twiggle village too.

"Why don't we take a picnic along so we don't get worried

1

if there aren't many nuts?" he suggested. "I always find that not having enough nuts makes me feel a bit peckish."

He was just about to start putting together a few delicious things when it turned out that Leaflette had already packed enough food for a huge feast.

So off they all went.

Twiggle expeditions are great fun to go on, if you love dancing. Everybody scampered this way and that doing picnic-type dances with trailing pink chiffon scarves.

Later on, as the merry villagers ambled through the dappled woods, they sang Twiggle songs with gentle melodies and fun choruses. Moss joined in with the choruses rather loudly because choruses are what Boggles do best.

The others didn't mind too much as long as he didn't join in every single song.

But when they reached their best nut trees there was a moment when everyone stopped dancing or singing all of a sudden, except for Moss who had got quite involved in the singing and had to be nudged twice by Leaflette to get him to shut up.

"What's wrong?" asked Moss.

"Look up at the trees!" His friends Oakum and Pippy were pointing upwards at the branches.

"Oh!" Moss gasped and he couldn't prevent making a hungry sort of gulping noise. Because, although these were definitely nut trees and it was certainly nut season, there didn't seem to be any nuts. Not a single one.

"There are a few bits of shell just here," said Oakum, staring at a pile of broken hazelnut shells on the ground.

Everyone looked very disappointed. There didn't seem to be much they could do about it though, so they decided to look elsewhere for food.

"Where should we go now to find nuts?" wondered Moss to a Twiggle named Willow who had been dancing nearby.

"I heard the very biggest ones are out beyond the Deep Reeds," replied Willow. "That's where the Witch gets them but Twiggles don't ever go that far."

"We went," Leaflette said proudly, "Swampy the Marsh Boggle, Moss and me, but it was very frightening. I'm not sure if I'd want to go there again. There's a very tricky broken bridge to cross."

Just then there was an alarming, crashing, clomping noise and the villagers all jumped into the nut-bushes to hide. Something really rather big was coming in their direction.

A huge spiky animal with enormous numbers of legs emerged from the gloom muttering to itself.

"It's okay," Moss shouted out in relief. "That's the Thornyclod. It's alright everyone, we know each other."

Slowly, all the Twiggles emerged from their bushes and began chatting about how they weren't at all frightened, just cautious, you know.

The Thornyclod looked like an enormous spiky spider with a different kind of shoe on each foot.

Moss and Leaflette went to say hello.

"Ah, it's young Leaflette and Moss. How are you? Thank you for the Wellington boot, it has lasted superbly." It waggled a back leg at the end of which was a purple boot. "A most fetching colour too. But where is your friend the Tree-Boggle?"

"Swampy is back home in the marshes," Moss explained, "though he is really a Marsh-Boggle not a Tree-Boggle."

"Well that would explain something then," said the Thornyclod. "He wouldn't have done well as a Tree Boggle. Kept falling out of them. He was terrible tree climber, you know," it explained to the gathering villagers who were a little alarmed but secretly rather pleased to meet a real live Thornyclod spider.

"Talking of trees, would you happen to know what has happened to all the nuts?" asked Oakum, who had to gather up lots of courage to talk to quite such a big creature.

"The nuts?" asked the Thornyclod. "That's what I've come for too. I've improved on my marshmallow recipe and now I add nuts. I'm a terribly keen cook, you see."

It looked very pleased with itself.

"But you can't have needed them all," argued Moss.

"No, no. Just a few. It isn't done to take the lot you know," said the Thornyclod. Then it began to look worried.

"I wonder if it could be those naughty little ruffians I met last time I was here." It had a long gloomy peer at the pile of nut shells.

Leaflette examined them too. "They've got teeth marks on them," she said. "Sharp ones. I have a nasty feeling these are bat bites. I think the bats might have taken all of the nuts."

"Why would the bats take them all?" wondered Moss. "They couldn't want to eat that many and we always leave some for the next people who might come along. Anyway, I didn't think bats ate nuts."

"Perhaps they have started to, now. I wonder what could have given them the idea?" mused Pippy.

"Ah well, I'll just be going then," announced the Thornyclod in a breezy manner and it began to lumber off. Moss stood in its way.

"Do you know why the bats took the nuts then?" he asked accusingly.

The Thornyclod shuffled in all its eight shoes. "It's not really my fault," it grumbled. "They all asked so many questions, you see."

It noticed that everyone was looking at it in a funny way. It coughed a little and finally it explained that a big gang of bats had caught it gathering nuts the week before and had found out that it was going to make nutmallows, which are like marshmallows only with nuts instead of marsh in them.

"I got confused and I think I might have told them the recipe," the Thornyclod sighed. "It was such a secret too. I don't think they knew you could eat them, up until then."

"Well, I suppose it's not really your fault," consoled

Leaflette. "You couldn't have guessed they would take the lot."

"Bats are very greedy. I should have thought of that before I told them. I bet they're terrible cooks too." The Thornyclod looked very depressed at the idea of all the nuts being wasted when it suddenly cheered up.

"I do know of another place where you can get nuts," it exclaimed. "The bats won't know about those bushes. I only know because the Witch told me."

"It's not beyond the Broken Bridge is it?" asked Leaflette. "Because if it is I don't think I could face another climb up there."

"That's where it is alright but we wouldn't have to climb," said the Thornyclod "I mean, do I look like a climbing kind of creature? I'm all legs up in the branches, you know. In fact, I'm very much a going-along-the-ground sort of person. But I am an excellent bush-basher. I've made a way through. If you like I'll show you all and we could swap recipes. I rather liked those barkicrisps you gave me."

"We'll teach you all the recipes we know," laughed Willow. "We would feel much safer to have you along. In fact, I don't think we'd feel scared at all."

So the Twiggle villagers followed the Thornyclod to the new nut trees and they chatted about food, dancing and singing as they went.

Moss discovered the Thornyclod knew a Boggle song or two and they sang them loudly together, because there aren't any Boggle songs you don't sing loudly. The Thornyclod had a very strange way of dancing to the beat, waggling each of its legs in turn. Boggles mostly just jump up and down at the really noisy moments.

Willow asked if she could hang her basket containing Sticklenose, the smallest of all the Twiggles, on one of the Thornyclod's spines and soon the gentle swaying motion put him straight to sleep. The sun was shining through the soft autumn leaves and even the dragonflies seemed to like the Twiggle dancing.

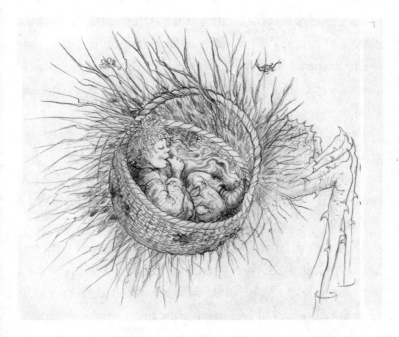

The High Climb

The Thornyclod was a very robust sort of traveller. It had a simple method of getting to where it wanted to go. It just plunged straight through all the bushes and undergrowth, often ignoring the paths altogether. After seeing it do this a couple of times, Willow decided Sticklenose might be safer if she carried him herself. This meant they had to go a bit slower. Even so it didn't take very long to reach the Broken Bridge.

Leaflette shivered a little when she saw the 'Be Bats' sign at the bottom of the bridge. She had seen it before. It had turned out to mean 'Beware of Bats' but a little bit of it had broken off. To her relief the Thornyclod didn't even look up at the high bridge in the trees.

"Follow me, little Twiggles. Onwards! Onwards!" it cried and it plunged through what had looked to Moss to be a very thick bush. When the villagers climbed through the hole the Thornyclod had made, they found to their surprise,

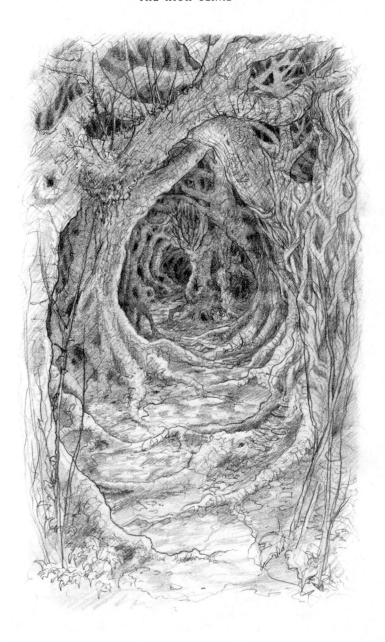

that they were in a long winding tunnel with its walls made from gnarled living branches. It twisted this way and that, avoiding the huge tree trunks on every side. There was hardly any light at all but somehow, with the Thornyclod clomping loudly through the dark tunnel and Moss singing, nobody felt scared. Soon they were travelling through much lighter undergrowth and the next thing they knew they were in a lovely, peaceful wood filled with birch trees and holly.

"The nut trees are over there," the Thornyclod said, pointing with two of its legs. And indeed they were. They were absolutely bursting with nuts. In fact there were so many that it only took a few minutes for the Twiggles to gather up all that they needed. Then they set out their

cooking things in a sunny clearing, and popped Sticklenose's basket in a shady place under a huge tree. They began to swap recipes with the Thornyclod.

It turned out that the Thornyclod didn't actually have many recipes, and the ones it did have mostly involved stomping on something and then stirring it in a pot.

"These feet aren't made for chopping things," it explained. "But they are great for cracking nuts."

So it taught the Twiggles about nutmallows in which the main ingredients were nuts and sugar. Then it explained its way of making biscuits with nuts and sugar. There was also a wonderful soup you could brew from nuts and sugar. All the same, the Twiggles agreed that everything tasted delicious. Then Willow made her nutbug crunch which turned out to be as scrumptious as ever.

Suddenly there was a great commotion and Willow was shouting, "No, Sticklenose, no! Come down! Now!"

Everybody rushed over to see what was happening.

"It's Sticklenose! He's up there!" cried Willow, pointing up into the trees.

Little baby Sticklenose had decided that, as it was his first party, he would celebrate by having his first tree-climb. He was making his way up a very tall tree using the tiniest of branches. No one could follow him because the twigs would snap. He was chortling happy noises as he climbed.

No matter what the Twiggles shouted out to him, Sticklenose resolutely kept on clambering upwards. A little

bit of blue sky had caught his eye and he wanted to get to it.

Twiggles, even little tiny ones, are born to climb and he was sure-footed on his journey, and because he was so light he could go where other Twiggles couldn't go. Soon enough, he was swaying happily at the absolute top of the tree. He made himself comfortable on a fork at the end of a thin branch and sat there cooing and gurgling.

Down below, there was pandemonium. Poor Willow was terribly upset and some of the other Twiggles were standing on each others' shoulders trying to get up the tree but it was no use.

They all tried to persuade him to climb back down but nothing worked.

Then Moss called up to the baby: "If you come down, Sticklenose, you can have all the sugar-twig clusters you like."

He waved a big sticky bag full of delicious sweets, which were still warm from being cooked. The gooey, sweet smell wafted up to the top of the tree and distracted Sticklenose who had been making gurgling noises at the leaves. He peered down from his twig cautiously. His big round eyes took one look at the journey to the sugar-twig cluster in Moss's hands. Much too difficult, he decided. He shook his head at the villagers below.

"Can't," he said mournfully. "Sticklenose stay here." He resumed his happy examination of the green leaves around him.

"If he can't get down then we'll have to go up somehow," Leaflette announced. "Can we build a ladder?"

But they couldn't build a ladder that would reach that high.

Then the Thornyclod announced that it had just had a tremendous idea: "If we can't climb up to him, then we'll have to fly there."

Even Moss looked at him a bit oddly. "We Boggles only do flying on the way down things, and I'm quite sure Thornyclods don't fly at all well, either."

"Of course we don't fly. What a silly idea. Much more sensible to stick to backwards and forwards only. If little Sticklenose had thought of that we'd all be better off. A

terribly silly idea for Thornyclods to start trying to fly, especially at my age, you know. As for Boggles and Twiggles flying…"

"If no one here can fly then it's not a very good idea," Moss said rather impatiently.

"Unless you happen to know someone who does know how to fly," said the Thornyclod, tapping its nose knowingly with a foot.

"Who is that?" they asked.

"Well, I happen to know the bats - slightly. They can fly."

Everyone looked dubious at this. Bats were definitely frightening and you never knew what scary things they would do.

"They might eat my baby," exclaimed Willow.

"I don't think they will today," the Thornyclod argued. "They'll be too stuffed with nutmallows."

Everyone began a very noisy discussion about what to do. But Moss pointed out they hadn't got any better ideas, so they decided to give it a go.

The Thornyclod, who knew where the bats lived, set off to find them. Willow asked if Moss and Leaflette would go along with the Thornyclod to make sure that it was going to be sensible. Which was very brave of them considering how frightened they were of bats.

The BeWILDerbats

The three wood dwellers had to go back through the dark tunnel and emerged right by the Broken Bridge.

"They live up there," the Thornyclod said, waggling a leg or two at the tree-tops. As they peered upwards they could make out lots of black bats swaying upside down in the highest branches. All three of them shouted up to try and get their attention, but none of the bats moved.

"Too full of nutmallows, I expect. Very greedy things, bats," muttered the Thornyclod.

"Perhaps we should climb up a bit so they can hear us," Leaflette suggested.

"Not me," said the Thornyclod decisively. "You two will have to go up alone."

"But the last time we did that they tried to eat us," Leaflette said nervously.

"Just shout the word 'Bewilderbats' to them as they fly about," the Thornyclod told them. "It's their gang name and

they won't attack you if you know that."

So Moss and Leaflette began to climb slowly up the tree to the Broken Bridge.

"What if they don't hear us when we shout Bewilderbats?" wondered Moss to Leaflette. He could tell by the way she trembled slightly that she had been thinking about that too. But when they got closer to the bats they were surprised to find that none of them stirred so much as a wing. Many of them were rocking gently and making soft groaning sounds.

"I suspect they've all eaten too much nutmallow," said Leaflette.

They called out to the gang and after they had shouted 'Bewilderbats' a few times the biggest bat opened one eye lazily.

"Who told you we were the Bewilderbats?" it asked.

"Our friend the Thornyclod," replied Leaflette.

"Who is terribly fierce!" added Moss, hoping that might make the bats think twice before eating them.

"No, it's not," said the bat, "and what is more it is a terrible cook. We've all got tummy-ache from a nutmallow recipe it gave us."

"Perhaps it's just because you ate too much," said Moss, who was still a bit annoyed that the bats had taken every single nut.

"Perhaps, perhaps not. Right then. Who are you and what do you want to talk about?" the bat asked.

So Moss and Leaflette introduced themselves and the bat told them it was the chief of the meanest gang of bats anywhere, and that it was called Snagglefang. Then they told him the story of Sticklenose and the tall tree.

"I don't think I can help you," Snagglefang said. "I'm supposed to be a fierce bat. I can't go about rescuing babies from trees. Next you'll be wanting me to feed your pet kittens."

The other bats muttered in agreement. Being in a tough gang and helping babies just didn't go together, they argued.

Just then Leaflette had a clever thought. "We Twiggles

know of something that will stop your tummy from hurting. If you help us, we could cure you in return."

"Hmm. It's true my tummy is just a little sore. Maybe it might not be too bad if it's only the one baby." Snagglefang rubbed his waist a little. It was very round and just a bit bumpy. The groans and moans from the other bats persuaded him.

"Alright, then. We'll do it. But first you'll have to pass the gang test," Snagglefang announced.

"Will it involve eating us?" asked Moss nervously.

"I don't think I'll try any Boggles today," said a big black bat called Beaker, patting an enormously round tummy. "No room."

"No eating you, then. Not this time. You'll have to answer a riddle though," Snagglefang said. "Ready?"

The two travellers nodded nervously.

"Right. What should you give an elf who wants to be taller?"

All the bats began to titter and giggle and Moss rubbed his chin thinking hard. But Snagglefang didn't give the two any time to reply, before he burst out with the answer.

"Elf raising flour!" he shouted, and he and all the other bats began shrieking with laughter.

"Elf raising flour, eh? That's a good one, that one," chortled a bat, clutching its sides and drying its eyes with a hanky.

"I've got one, I've got one," called Beaker. "What do you get if you pour boiling water down a rabbit hole? Hmm? I'll

tell you. You get hot cross bunnies!" The bats shrieked once more with hilarity.

"Two chances gone then. I'll give you both just one more chance," offered Snagglefang. "We'll do a knock knock riddle. You start."

"Knock, Knock," said Moss, confused.

"Who's there?" asked Snagglefang giggling, sniggering under his wing.

Moss said nothing as he didn't know. Suddenly there was an eerie silence.

"I'm not absolutely sure I got that one quite right," muttered Snagglefang after a short while. Then he clapped his wings. "Right they've passed the test. We had better be off rescuing babies," and with loud cries of "'Bewilderbats' rule!" a great cloud of black wings dropped off their branches and headed towards Sticklenose's tree.

Moss and Leaflette climbed down to let the Thornyclod know what happened.

"You didn't tell them about the nut trees did you?" it asked anxiously. They reassured it that they hadn't.

"Perhaps they won't see them" it thought to itself, hopefully, as they travelled back to the others.

The Wise Witch

When Moss and Leaflette got back to the picnic site, they found Sticklenose still sitting at the top of the tree. He didn't seem in the least bit upset, but he didn't seem any more likely to climb down. The bats looked much better, probably because it had done their tummies good to get out in the fresh air.

Snagglefang, the chief of the Bewilderbats, was explaining the situation to the Twiggles. "We've been up and chatted to him and he does seem to be a nice little chap. He even laughed at one of my jokes. But we can't get him down for you."

"Why not? Will he have to stay up there forever?" wailed Willow, looking most alarmed.

"Well, he'll have to stay up there for now because there are too many branches all about him for us to fly him out. We'd drop him if we hit our wings on them. But we have decided that as he is such an excellent fellow, we'll make

him a member of the gang and then we can bring him food to eat."

"Please take him his little hat," added Willow. "He'll be getting chilly up there."

The bats were unsure if wearing bobble hats suited a tough new member of the Bewilderbats gang, especially as it was so warm, but after one look at Willow's determined face, they decided to agree.

So things were improving, but Sticklenose was still stuck. Just as they were all discussing the best thing to do next, there was a sort of shimmering light in the clearing and then a pretty little robin was flitting about above their heads. Following the small red-breasted bird came a witch

27

carrying a basket of flowers and herbs.

"I heard there was a bit of trouble in this part of Bewilderwood, so I came to see if I could help," she announced. It was the Witch of Bewilderwood. She looked after all the creatures in the forest.

The Twiggles were delighted to see her as she was a friendly sort of witch, if you were a friendly sort of Twiggle. The bats however looked worried. There had been a bit of business last week when they had taken all of the scrubbleroot the witch was growing to make her special potions, and she had been quite cross. Not only that but scrubbleroot soup turned out to taste very nasty and bitter.

They all hoped nobody would mention the matter of the nuts to her.

The Witch listened to the villagers as they explained Sticklenose's problem and she thought about it for a bit.

"Well," she said, "if he can't climb down and he can't fly down then I think he'll just have to jump down."

"But he'll be squished flat," protested Willow.

"Not if you stretch a net below him. Then he'll be safe," suggested the Witch.

Everyone was very excited. It seemed so obvious when she said it, that they wondered why they hadn't thought of it earlier. Moss was particularly pleased as the bats were taking a lot more food up to Sticklenose than seemed healthy for a baby of his size, and he was worried about the supplies running out.

Leaflette pointed out a slight problem. They hadn't got a net.

"The Thornyclod is a spider. It could make one," suggested Pippy.

The Thornyclod looked embarrassed. "I've never really got the hang of weaving nets you know. All left feet I'm afraid. I could make a huge bowl of marshmallows and he could jump into that, if you like," it suggested.

Willow said that she wasn't going to have her baby get quite that sticky and that was that.

Just then the Witch spoke: "I know where you could get some strong thread. The Slitherigrubs weave very strong nets and they would be happy to help, I'm sure. They live in the Black Marshes just beyond my house. You could go there and be back before evening if you like. I'm going that way so we could travel together for a while."

Moss shivered a little because a trip to the Black Marshes was not what he had hoped for on a pretty summer's day. There were strange things in there and something which made horrible howls.

"Don't worry Moss," smiled the Witch. "Scrop will protect you."

Moss shivered quite a bit more. He wondered who (or what) Scrop might be.

Just then Snagglefang made things more complicated.

"We're a gang of bats, not babysitters. We can't spend all day here looking after a bobble-hatted baby, even if he is quite good at getting riddles," he said.

"We told him that one about where the king kept his armies," Beaker said, as one or two of the other bats started shuffling about behind him, giggling under their wings. "He thought that joke very funny. In fact he was laughing so much that he got hiccoughs."

"Next we'll show him how to sleep upside down in the trees," suggested a small bat, but Willow said she didn't think this was a good idea at all.

"If we make you more of the tummy-ache potion for later, will you stay and help?" Leaflette asked craftily. "Then you would be alright when you have another feast."

"We'd definitely stay if you did that. As long as you keep feeding Sticklenose lots of that delicious nutbug crunch," said Snagglefang, helping himself to a very large basketful of sweets.

Willow gave him a little reed hammock for Sticklenose's nap time, in case any of the bats were silly enough to try to teach him to sleep upside down.

So it was agreed, and the Twiggles chose Moss, Leaflette and Pippy for the adventure. They set about gathering the things that the three would need for the journey.

"How do you know if nutbug crunch is delicious if only Sticklenose had some?" Moss suddenly asked the bats suspiciously. But no one was listening.

The three travellers set off towards the Scary Lake on their way to the Black Marshes. As they walked the noise of the picnic faded into the distance. The last thing they could hear was Beaker, the bat explaining the joke to Snagglefang.

"He keeps them in his sleevies. Get it? Get it? Armies. In his sleevies. Ha! Ha!"

Then they were walking through the tall swaying reeds, with Rosie the robin twittering happily on Moss's shoulder.

The Toothy Tour

After a while the gently waving reeds gave way to ripe bullrushes and tall green marshy plants. The bullrushes were just ready to burst and the air was full of their fluffy white seeds floating about.

"I think we will get there quicker if we ask Mildred the Crocklebog to give us a lift," the Witch suggested. "Let's go and find her."

They followed the Witch deeper and deeper through the fronds and entangled marsh trees. Soon they were at the water's edge.

"Why don't you get Mildred's attention while I slip off to pick some useful flowers," said the Witch.

Over by the far side of the lake an enormous spiny Crocklebog was rushing about in the water. She was chasing after a panic-struck coot which was dodging this way and that. Finally the coot got safely to the side of the lake and scuttled off. Mildred seemed to calm down a bit.

When Pippy saw the great spiky creature he wondered if it was such a good idea to be going on this adventure. Only they had to rescue Sticklenose.

"It's huge and it has an awful lot of teeth. Is it quite safe?" he asked.

"Oh that's alright," laughed Moss and Leaflette. "She's vegetarian, you see. We should gather some reeds to sit on, because her back is quite thorny."

They called out to her: "Hi Mildred! Hello! Hello! It's us."

It took a while to distract Mildred from chasing butterflies but finally she heard them.

"It'th Moth and Leaflette! Ooh goody, goody! Hello!"

She snorted happily and swam over with her long tail swishing behind her. She seemed very excited to see them, but just as she was getting close there was a sort of explosion. Suddenly two huge jets of water shot out of her nose and drenched the three travellers - and also the Witch who was just returning.

"Whoopth! Thorry," said Mildred. "I thometimeth do that when I'm happy to catch up with friendth. Ooh Hello!"

Another smaller spray drenched Pippy again who Mildred had just noticed.

"Hello. I'm Mildred and I'm a Thorny Crocklebog. From a long line of other Crocklebogth like me. And I've got a lithp which makes me talk funny but I think it maketh me thound friendly. Who are you? Will you be friendth? The cooth won't, I'm afraid."

Once Pippy had got over his alarm and dried himself down, he explained who he was.

"Thorry if I made you all wet," she smiled uneasily at the Witch.

"That's alright. We'll be dry in a bit," said the Witch, "especially if you would be so kind as to take us on your back to the Boggle village where we could borrow some new clothes."

"Delighted," smiled Mildred.

After Pippy had helped collect the reeds, they arranged them into comfortable seats on Mildred's back and set off across the shimmering water.

Swampy's Mum

Everyone was quiet as they swished gently across the lake. The travellers were enjoying the lovely ride, and Mildred was wondering just what sort of food she might like best when they got there. She was hoping that Swampy's mum would be at home as she was an excellent cook. Maybe she would have some clunknettle soup. It was just the right season for it.

She licked her teeth thoughtfully and slid gracefully into the channel which led to the Boggle village. There was a lovely marshy smell and bubbles were bursting in the muddy shallows. All around were lots of dragonflies flitting this way and that in a complicated dance. The bullrushes were almost bursting, and there were large fruit bushes weighed down with delicious red fruit. They picked some as a present for Swampy's mum.

They arrived at the fishing pond which the Boggles liked to use, and as they were crossing it they spied a boat on the other side with four feet poking sleepily over its edge. Mildred swished slowly up to the little craft. "Hello," she snorted, happily. "Oh blatht! I've done it again."

Two very surprised and wet Boggles emerged from the bottom of the boat where they had been having a mid-morning kip.

"It's Swampy!" cried Leaflette and Moss. "How lovely to see you again."

Swampy emptied his hat of water and smiled back at them.

"Hello everyone!" he said. "Thank you for the bath Mildred. I wasn't due to have mine for a week, but I suppose I won't have to now."

Mildred looked a bit embarrassed.

Then Swampy introduced everyone to Marsha, the pretty Boggle girl sitting next to him. They shook each others' hands.

"We're going on a big adventure to save Baby Sticklenose. Are you coming?" asked Pippy.

"Ah," Swampy said. "A big adventure? I've had one of those before, you see, and what with getting lunch for Mum and everything…"

"I've caught enough fish to make lunch for your mum," interrupted Marsha. "I know you'd rather go adventuring and meeting terrible monsters and things."

"We're off to find some Slitherigrubs," Moss said.

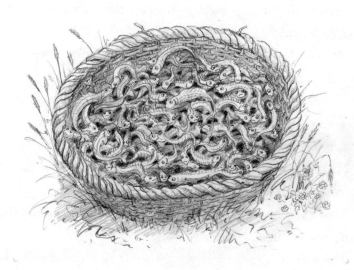

"Swampy is so brave," said Marsha to the others. "I know he'd love to find Slitherigrubs with you, but I have to get back. I must finish mending my dress for the village feast. Oh, and I must give these to Swampy's mum."

She held up a basket of long Slimifish which were still slithering and wriggling.

"Are Slitherigrubs scary?" Swampy wondered in a just-thought-I'd-ask sort of way.

"No, no. They're brilliant at weaving nets and the Witch says they're friendly," Leaflette replied. The Witch confirmed this with a smile.

They explained about Sticklenose and the bats and Swampy scratched his nose a little before deciding.

"Well, perhaps one more adventure won't hurt. Alright, I'll come along," he agreed.

"We aught to give Swampy's mum these roseberries we picked for her," said Moss.

"And we should dry our clothes on the washing lines," the Witch pointed out sensibly.

"Do you think your mum would let me have any clunknettle thoup?" Mildred asked Swampy excitedly. Another small spout of water splashed the boat.

"I'm sure she would," said Swampy as he used his hat to scoop water out of the bottom of his boat.

They then headed back to the village. Marsha joined the gang on Mildred's back.

The way to the Boggle village went through the lovely

fishing ponds, which were lined with silvery willows. The muddy water plopped lazily with little bubbles rising between the great green water-lily leaves. Brightly coloured butterflies flickered across the water, and a red and blue kingfisher chirped hello to them as they passed.

Then they were at the village in the reeds. Swampy tied his boat up to the jetty, while Mildred's passengers clambered off her back and started to climb up the spiral stairs to the houses.

Swampy's mum was hanging out her washing in the warm breeze when she saw them. She waved to Mildred who waved back enthusiastically with both hands. This time no one got wet.

Mildred looked at the narrow stairs for quite a while before deciding that she would prefer to stay where she was in the water.

"There's a huge pot of clunknettle soup up here, which we are making for the big feast." Swampy called down from the village platform. "We'll bring some down to you." Swampy's mum looked a little pleased not to have quite such a watery animal in the village on washing day, but as she was very fond of Mildred she came down the steps herself, carrying a great big steaming bowl of soup.

To be sociable everyone joined Mildred on the jetty. They were wrapped up in big warm blankets while their clothes dried out.

After Mildred had a small second helping, they checked

the clothes and found that they were almost dry. Marsha had to say goodbye because she had lots of work to do for the big party. She promised, however, to make Mildred a jaunty pink hat if she would come as her special guest.

Then the Witch gave a little cough and said: "It's a long way to the Black Marshes so I think you'd better get on your way."

Swampy went very pale at the mention of the Black Marshes. He'd been there before and something in there had made peculiar howling noises. He turned round very quickly to see if Marsha wanted his help instead, but she had already gone.

"Shall we all go in my boat?" he asked.

"Perhaps Mildred could take you there," proposed the Witch. "She is exactly the right shape. Just go down the Dismal Dyke over there. It will lead you all the way to the Black Marshes."

"Ooh yeth!" Mildred enthused. "I know I'll love the Dark Marsheth and I bet there will be loadth of friendly creatures to make friendth with."

It didn't seem to Swampy that going down the Dismal Dyke was actually an adventure. It seemed more a sort of punishment. But, he reasoned, if they were travelling with the Witch it was bound to be safe.

"I hope there are a few nice bits and bobs to eat," he said eventually.

"Certainly," the Witch said. "I'll leave you all my food as

I've got to go and pay a visit to a friend nearby and I'm sure she'll have something good to eat. Maybe even a bowl of that delicious smelling soup. Well, good luck, all of you."

"Aren't you coming along with us?" exclaimed Swampy.

Before he could try and persuade her there was a sort of shimmering effect in the light and she suddenly wasn't there anymore.

"Gulp!" went someone, and none of the travellers could be completely sure it wasn't them.

The Slitherigrubs

The entrance to the Dismal Dyke is not easy to find and when you do find it you might prefer that you hadn't.

Eventually Leaflette announced: "I think this must be it."

The Boggles and Twiggles stared through a blackened arch, formed by an ancient thorn bush, at a slimy green passage of narrow water. It was enclosed in a tunnel of branches and spiky plants. Strange, dark, wet leaves were dripping from above.

"Well, thith lookth like fun," said Mildred, but she didn't sound very cheery. It wasn't the sort of place any of them really wanted to go. Then they remembered Sticklenose, so Mildred began to move very slowly along the waterway.

The sun vanished and it suddenly felt much colder. The dangling dark leaves dripped cold slimy drops of water down the back of their necks. Creatures in the spiny undergrowth made spooky clicking noises and there wasn't any birdsong.

The travellers all huddled much closer together.

"It'th not a very friendly kind of plathe," said Mildred gloomily. The others quivered a little on her back.

The dark water seemed to be leading them left and right and left again. The trees seemed even bigger, and the sky even further away. Soon the only sounds were little watery plinks as drops fell from the branches above.

"I wonder what my mum would have cooked for us if we'd stayed at home," said Swampy. His voice seemed to echo in the darkness.

Mildred made a moaning noise and shivered so hard that all four had to hold on to her spines tightly.

Then Pippy pointed something out: "The water doesn't go on any further. I think we've found the edge of the Black Marshes. We'll have to go on by foot now."

The four of them looked nervously at the dark muddy thicket ahead.

Mildred cleared her throat a little and tiny plumes of water spurted out of her nose.

"I'm a thwimming thort of Crocklebog really and there aren't any friendth to make here. If it'th alright with you I'll drop you off and go back."

"Of course, Mildred," said Leaflette. "Thank you so much for taking us this far. Will you be okay in the dark on your own?"

"I think I will. Ath long ath I keep thinking of all the yummy food Thwampy'th mum might give me to eat," she said enthusiastically, and she splashed about a bit patting her tummy.

The others looked a little downhearted as they climbed out at the edge of the water. They watched Mildred slide gently back down the Dismal Dyke.

"I'll meet you at the nextht party," she called back. "I'll put a thcrumy Crocklebog treat or two in my handbag for you."

If they were going to have to have a scary adventure it seemed a good idea not to be hungry too, so they unpacked the food that the Witch had given them. There were some delicious treats in there. At the top was a really good sweetsludge pie, and then there were some powderleaf

pasties, and a tin full of delicious mudwort jelly.

Everybody cheered up immediately and tucked in. After a while Swampy licked some jelly off his fingers and said, "I bet Mildred would have liked this jelly."

"Yes, a terrible pity she had to go back," Moss replied helping himself to another large mouthful.

"Maybe we'd better go and find some Slitherigrubs now," Pippy suggested. "I wonder, what do they look like?"

They all stared at each other. No one had thought to ask the Witch that.

"Also, without Mildred, we will have to find our way through the Black Marshes," Swampy pointed out gloomily.

"Maybe we'll meet someone we can ask," Leaflette suggested hopefully.

There wasn't any other choice so the four friends set off timidly into the Black Marshes. They had to pick their way round all kinds of murky, muddy pools and gnarled broken trees and with every step it got deeper and darker.

After a while, Swampy spoke: "Does anyone know what those funny lights are over there?" he asked.

They looked in the direction he was pointing. There were hundreds of spooky glowing lights hanging from the trees. Some were green, some an eerie pink and some were a weird shade of orange.

"It looks a very peculiar place," muttered Pippy nervously. "I don't think we should go there without the Witch to protect us."

"I don't think we have any choice," Moss pointed out. "It's the only way that isn't through those really horrible looking marshes."

They edged closer to the creepy lights. Soon they were glowing all around them. From every branch dangled lots of silvery mossy strands which often brushed against their faces. They found to their relief that the ground was much harder here, and if it weren't so spooky Leaflette might have thought the place rather beautiful in an eerie kind of way.

"Look!" shouted Moss suddenly. "I can see some higher land over there. I think it might be the way out!"

Everyone looked terribly relieved, especially Pippy, who had just been discussing with Swampy whether they might have to spend the night here. A shudder slithered up and down his back at the idea.

"Let's go over there then," Swampy said, quickening his step.

"But we haven't met the Slitherigrubs. We can't go back unless we've got a net for poor little Sticklenose," Leaflette reminded them. This made everyone stop and think.

"Perhaps another small bite might help us think of how to find them," suggested Moss hopefully.

So they unpacked the food again as sometimes even quite a small snack can make you feel much braver.

"I don't like all those silver creepy things on all the branches," said Swampy through a mouthful of sweetsludge

pie. "They get on your face like spider's webs, only they are slimy. Ughh!" and he shivered again.

Then Leaflette jumped up and pulled hard on one of the dangling damp strands. She suddenly started laughing and did a little Twiggle dance around the others.

"Well done, you've got it Swampy! You are so clever." She hugged the surprised Boggle. Swampy looked both pleased and confused.

"What have I got?" he asked.

"The answer to where the Slitherigrubs are, of course. It was you saying about spider's webs that made me realise. These slimy things are the Slitherigrub's threads. All those glowing things are the grubs themselves. This means we can

save little Sticklenose now!"

They looked around and saw that each light was actually the tail of some fat whitish grub hanging from threads attached to the branches. They didn't seem to talk, but they all had friendly peaceful expressions on their faces.

Pippy pulled down a long strand without a grub on the end. "I think these ones are old. I'm sure they won't mind us using them."

Soon they had gathered enough of the damp threads to weave a huge net. They decided to make for higher land in the hope it would lead them out of the Black Marshes.

The Crooked Shack

The tall woods were very gloomy and the sky seemed a long way away. At first there were a few dank, wet, marshy pools but the further they went the more squelchy it became. Finally, they were travelling through nothing but black muddy swamp.

The Boggles were much better at finding the safest way to go than the Twiggles, who really preferred to be in trees, so Swampy and Moss went first. They tried a bit of singing but they found that it wasn't so fun if your voice is a bit trembly, so they just travelled quietly after that.

Even a wise Boggle can get a bit lost if the marshes are thick enough, and these ones were very thick indeed. Swampy sat on a spiky tussock and after he had stood up and rubbed his trouser seat a little, he admitted to Moss that he wasn't absolutely sure they were going in the right direction.

Pippy suggested he climb a tree to see if he could see

where they should head next. They saw him climb up a
dripping dark trunk to the very top.

"I can't see any high land but there are some orange
lights over that way," he called down, pointing with his arm.
"Maybe someone lives there who will help us?"

Swampy wondered if he really wanted to be helped by
anyone who lived in the Black Marshes. Still, it seemed like
a good idea to at least find out what the lights were.

Soon they all could see the radiant orange glow shining
through the sedge leaves, but they were partly hidden
by very thick bushes. The four intrepid travellers inched
cautiously to the edge of the bushes, and they saw something
which made even Leaflette gulp. There were lots of orange

55

pumpkins with horrible toothy grins standing on poles, and they were all lit up inside with a strange unnatural light. Even the strange Slitherigrubs had seemed less frightening than this. There was something else too. They could just make out a black wooden shack with a wonky chimney a little beyond the lanterns.

"I don't care what anyone says, I'm not going to go and talk to anyone who lives in that," Moss declared quietly. "It's even got a big cooking pot over there which could fit all of us in." Everyone else stared silently.

"Let's go back and find a path around it if we can," suggested Pippy.

They were just about to do exactly that when they heard a noise in the marsh behind them. There are some noises which are nice to hear in scary places, like a friend shouting "anyone for chocosticks?" or just a snatch of Boggle singing. There are other noises which most Boggles and Twiggles would much rather not hear, and this was one of those sorts of noises. It started as a kind of roaring, groaning sound and ended with a high pitched screech. The four found that they had jumped into a tiny huddle together and were trying to look as small as possible. Moss seemed to be trying to dig a hole.

"Wh..what was that?" whispered Leaflette nervously.

"It sounds like something that would definitely eat Boggles," Moss suggested in a quavering voice.

"I remember the Witch said Scrop would protect us," said

Pippy, hopefully. "Let's hope that Scrop gets here before that thing does."

They wondered to themselves who (or what) Scrop was and how (or why) it would help.

They listened carefully as they hid in the bushes. Nothing. Then there was another roar much, much closer. They huddled together, terrified. Just as Swampy was wondering if knocking on the door of the shack might be better than being eaten up, there was an even louder roar, and a horrible bashing sound coming towards them.

"It's coming our way! Run! Run!" shouted Moss.

The four travellers shot out of the bushes and sprinted right past all the spooky pumpkins, past the big black pot, and past the creaking shack. They kept on running as fast as possible, but they could hear the thing behind trying to catch up with them.

Then, at last, the ground changed from black swamp to rustling leaves and the light began to flood in through the high branches. They were finally on high land. Whatever it was that was chasing them seemed to prefer it in the marsh. It made a mournful howling noise, and lumbered slowly away into the blackness, moaning.

The Boggles and Twiggles found their legs had become a bit wobbly so they all sat down, panting.

Swampy mopped his brow with his hat with such relief that he forgot to ask if anyone still had any food. But it turned out that Leaflette hadn't dropped the bundle of delicious things the Witch had given them, so they settled down to finish it off.

The Wobbly Wire

"I wonder where we are, because this place seems familiar to me," Swampy said to the others as he cleaned his teeth with a twig.

"I think you are right, Swampy. We've both been here before," agreed Leaflette. "Isn't this where we met the Witch on our last adventure? It's very near the Far Tree."

"Perhaps that shack thing is where she lives. And that pot is her cauldron," suggested Moss.

"I think you're right, but I wonder why she has all those scary pumpkins and things," said Swampy.

"Well, she is a witch. I'm sure she has a reason," said Leaflette. "Anyway, we know the way back from here, so let's take our Slitherigrub threads to the picnic grounds and rescue Sticklenose."

"The Broken Bridge is to the west," pointed out Moss. "If we go towards the sun, we'll get there soon enough."

So they travelled through the autumn trees as the warm

gentle sun soothed away all the nasty memories of the Black Marshes. They sang songs to the butterflies and birds, which fluttered and flitted in the branches, and altogether they made a much jollier party than before.

As they wandered through the woods, the leafy ground became a little hilly. Pippy and Leaflette danced on ahead and the two slower Boggles followed behind them swapping jokes that they thought the Bewilderbats might like. As they chatted and laughed, they hardly noticed that they were climbing up a gentle slope.

Swampy was just finishing a favourite joke when he noticed Pippy rushing back to talk to them. He looked very worried.

"Hello, Pippy. Is anything wrong?" asked Swampy.

"I think so. There's a cliff up ahead and I don't think you'd be able to climb down it," said Pippy. "Leaflette has managed it but now she can't get back up and I can't find a way around. What shall we do?"

They ran after Pippy to the place where Leaflette had climbed down, but he was right. It was much too dangerous for Boggles to climb down. Leaflette had only succeeded because she was an elegant Twiggle and Twiggles spend their lives climbing. But she had jumped the last bit and she wasn't tall enough to climb back up.

Boggles don't generally have a lot of brilliant ideas. Mostly when Swampy thought he had one, everybody else thought he didn't. But this time he thought of something really clever.

"Why don't we tie all the Slitherigrub threads together and make a rope and rescue her?" he suggested.

"Did you really think of that all on your own?" Moss asked, very impressed.

Swampy tried to look modest but went a bit red in the face.

The three of them tied enough Slitherigrub rope to reach Leaflette. But there was a lot left over, as Slitherigrubs make the strongest and thinnest rope in all of Bewilderwood.

They lowered it down to Leaflette who caught the other end. Instead of climbing up it, she shouted back to the others: "Can you make it even longer? If you do, I think there's a way we can all get to the bottom safely."

So they worked busily and soon Leaflette had a big coil of rope at her feet while Moss held the other end.

"Tie your end to a really strong tree," she shouted up.

So Moss tied his end to a big stump, as Leaflette suggested and they watched as she ran off into the distance with the other end. She found another tree a long way away and, after pulling the rope tight, the Boggles saw she had made a long rope line stretching downwards at a gentle angle.

She cupped her hands around her mouth to make her voice bigger, and they heard her distant voice calling: "You have to find a V-shaped twig. If you put it over the rope and hold both sides then you can slide all the way down."

Swampy and Moss had done this before so they found just the right sticks. Pippy was looking very nervous.

"It's alright. Watch us go first. It's easy once you are brave enough to jump off," smiled Moss to Pippy.

He took his twig, looped it over the line and, holding both ends, whizzed happily all the way down to Leaflette. He made a lot of noise, shouting and whooping as he went. Boggles can't help being noisy when they are really having fun.

Then it was Swampy's turn. He loved it just as much, and it took a while for the cheery echoes to die down.

They looked high up the cliff only to see Pippy looking downwards suspiciously.

"Are you sure it's safe and the rope won't break?" Pippy asked in a slightly squeaky voice.

"If it can take a Boggle the size of Swampy, I'm sure a slender Twiggle like you will be fine," called back Leaflette reassuringly.

Pippy stood for a few moments at the top of the line, and then he took a deep breath and jumped.

"Wow! Wheee!" he shouted. "This is the best fun ever!"

They decided to leave the rope tied to the trees in case anyone needed it another time. There was easily enough rope left over to make Sticklenose's net.

As they travelled through the pine forest to get to the Broken Bridge, Leaflette noticed that Swampy was looking at his tummy very carefully.

"It's not that I'm all that big a Boggle, you know. It's just that food has a sort of way of making friends with me," he explained to Leaflette.

"Oh Swampy!" she laughed and gave him a huge hug. "You are just exactly the size an idea-having Boggle like you should be."

Swampy looked very pleased at that and rubbed his tummy proudly.

The Daring Dive

The four brave adventurers arrived in the picnic clearing to great fuss and attention.

"Thank you so much for getting the rope for my little Sticklenose," said a tearful Willow. "Was it dangerous?"

Just as Swampy was about to explain the whole story, Leaflette said, "We'd better start making the net first and Swampy will tell you the whole tale as we weave it. He's the best storyteller of all of us. But first, how is Sticklenose?"

"He's very well, I think," said Willow. "But he does seem to be eating an awful lot of nutbug crunch, and I worry that he might remember some of the jokes those bats have told him. They seem to have made friends up there."

They settled down to tie the net, and Swampy began to tell the strange tale of how they had found the Slitherigrubs and of the terrible noises in the swamps. He spent quite a long time when it came to his clever idea about the rope but everyone listened carefully.

Soon the net was finished.

Snagglefang came to make sure the net was being hung in the right place for Sticklenose to jump into it. Some of the other bats did funny imitations of Twiggles dancing and all the villagers laughed at them.

Suddenly Moss shouted: "Look, some of the bats are stealing all our nutbug crunch!"

They turned and saw Beaker and two smaller bats shuffling away from the food basket looking guilty.

"If we rescue Sticklenose safely, I'll cook you all the nutbug crunch you want," said Willow generously.

At that moment the Witch arrived. No one ever really knew how she would always suddenly appear just when she

was needed but, they were very glad to see her.

She checked the net to make sure it was strong enough, and then it was time for Sticklenose to jump.

Snagglefang flew up to the tree-top to make sure he knew what to do.

They chatted for a while and Willow was quite sure that he was telling Sticklenose another unsuitable joke.

Then Sticklenose stood up on the branch.

"Do be careful, dear," shouted Willow.

Sticklenose raised both arms slowly above his head and then did a graceful swan-dive right into the middle of the net.

The next minute he was being squeezed in one of the biggest hugs in Twiggle history.

"You're safe, darling Sticklenose!" Willow was saying over and over.

They all rushed off to congratulate Swampy and the others and to thank the Witch. Everyone seemed very happy and noisy when Snagglefang suddenly shouted.

"Stop that Sticklenose! Stop!" he cried.

Sticklenose was half way back up the tree and heading for the sky again.

"One tiny, tiny jumpy?" he pleaded but Oakum had already climbed up the tree to get him. He tucked Sticklenose safely under his arm and returned him to his mother.

The Witch hadn't heard about the big adventures of Swampy, Pippy, Moss and Leaflette so they sat on the

warm grass and told her what they had found in the Black Marsh.

Pippy wanted to know why she had so many strange glowing pumpkins behind her house.

"Oh, I let some of the older Slitherigrubs retire in my Halloween pumpkins. They make just enough rope for me to keep the FarTree stocked with shoes for any travellers who might need them," she smiled. "Also it means I can see at night if I'm brewing a potion and need some herbs from the garden."

Pippy was a little surprised to hear of the creepy Black Marshes being described as a garden.

"Scrop was sorry that you didn't wait for him to say hello," she added.

"We were running away from something horrible and noisy," pointed out Swampy.

"Yes, he said he tried to run after you but you were just too quick for you. You must have been running very fast," said the Witch.

"Does that mean the thing we were running from was really only Scrop?" exclaimed Moss. "I thought it was going to eat us up."

"Goodness me, no! He wouldn't find Boggles or Twiggles at all to his taste," laughed the Witch. Then she peered over Leaflette's shoulder. "Whatever are those pesky bats up to now?"

Snagglefang and Beaker were sneaking off with what was

left of the Slitherigrub's rope. They explained that they were going to make hammocks with them as they didn't always like to have to sleep upside down. They had got the idea from the one Willow had sent up to Sticklenose.

"It's nice to have a change of position once in a while. We've already made some Marshmallow cushions for our heads," said Snagglefang.

"Uh, oh!" muttered Beaker. "I think I might have eaten those."

Snagglefang glared at him.

"If you want things you have to ask for them. You shouldn't just take them anyway," said the Witch. "I don't want to have to cast a spell to make you behave better."

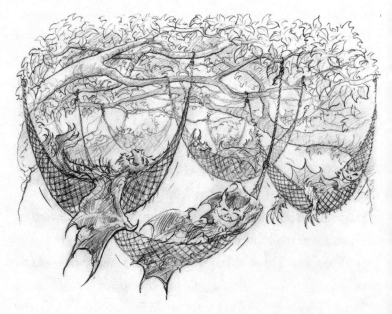

"No, no, we'll be good now," said both bats in unison, backing away from the Witch slowly.

"Well, just to make sure, I've got an idea which will mean you won't be able to play with Sticklenose until you learn better manners. I've suggested that the Twiggles build a little play village in the pines where the trees aren't so tall. I'm going to ban the bats if they aren't well behaved. It's right by my house so I can keep an eye on the toddler Twiggles from there."

"We could call it Toddlewood-on-the-Hill," said Willow looking very pleased. "Sticklenose would love it there."

"We will try to be better, and we'll ask first before we take things, but we're still the 'Bewilderbats'," said Snagglefang. "We're a fierce gang of bats and we wouldn't go near Tiddlerwood anyway. Although I will admit that little Sticklenose can join our gang any time he likes."

Sticklenose smiled at that, but he looked at Snagglefang with his big eyes.

"No more stealies then?" he said seriously.

Snagglefang held his hand. "We'll always ask first," he promised. Sticklenose gave him a big grin.

Then Snagglefang turned to face his group of shame-faced bats. "Right you lot. We've done our work here. It's back to the woods for us," he growled.

"But Willow promised to make us lots of nutbug crunch after we rescued Sticklenose," complained Beaker.

"And I never told the delightful little fellow the answer

to my joke about what you give to a sick pig," said another bat.

"I know. You give it oinkment," said Beaker and all the bats began falling about with laughter, slapping each other on the back and guffawing.

"Come on you rabble. Home!" ordered Snagglefang and the bats took off in a great black crowd and headed for the treetops.

"Thanks so much for saving my boy," called Willow after them. "I'll make you some nutbug crunch as soon as I get home."

The
BeWILDerparty

The Twiggles and the Boggles worked very hard to make a safe place for the younger ones to have fun. It had slides and swings and little tiny houses and even a roly-poly hill to tumble down. When the Witch came to visit, she said it looked so good that they deserved to have a huge party.

"We should have it right here so that all the little Twiggles and Boggles can have somewhere to play.

The bats may have been very naughty, but they really helped with Sticklenose. Let's ask them too," Willow suggested.

So that evening a wonderful spread of all the food you could imagine was laid out. There was a huge sweetsludge pie, and barkicrisps, and mudwort jelly made especially by the Witch. The Thornyclod brought along its best ever marshmallows, flavoured delicately with delicious marsh and, of course, Willow made her famous nutbug crunch.

Mildred brought some crocklechocs she had cooked for

the party. She looked wonderful in her brand new pink hat which Marsha had made her. There was also a lovely matching pink handbag with a purple patch sewn on it to set it off. She joined in a big gang of Twiggles to discuss everyone's outfits.

"But I think I like mine the betht," she said firmly.

The dancing began to start and soon the woods were filled with the happy sight of Twiggles trailing chiffon scarves through the trees and Boggles dancing on their heads waving their legs in the air. Down below Mildred was galumphing gaily in the nearby marsh.

Then Oakum pointed to the sky.

"It's the 'Bewilderbats'," he cried out happily.

"Ooh goody!" shouted Mildred and a great muddy arc of water shot from her nose and soaked poor Beaker who was flying just above her. He said it was such a nice party that he didn't mind at all.

Then the bats gave a stunning show of synchronised flying. There were only one or two small accidents.

When the bats landed, all the Villagers gathered around them to thank them for their help. They gave each of them a gift of a small hammock made from Slitherigrub thread, so no one would have to sleep upside down if they didn't want to.

Beaker made a long speech of thanks but he stopped when he noticed everyone had wandered off to eat more scrummy food. He decided to join them.

The villagers noticed that the Bewilderbats did eat rather a lot but they didn't steal anything and everyone laughed loudly at their riddles.

Snagglefang sat next to Sticklenose and wrapped a wing around his shoulders. The two of them swapped jokes all night.

Finally, it was time for everyone to go home so Swampy said goodbye to Moss and Leaflette and Willow gave the last of the nutbug crunch to Beaker.

Snagglefang gave Sticklenose a big hug. "I'll miss you, little fellow," he said. "Come and visit soon."

Sticklenose waved goodbye to the big friendly bat and he kept on waving until Snagglefang was just a tiny black dot in the sky.

Then Willow took him home.

The End

Discover the other books in the magical

BeWILDerwood

range!

A Boggle at BeWILDerwood
Follow Swampy as he leaves the comfort of his own marsh and journeys into the magical world of BeWILDerwood on a thrilling and daring adventure that proves he's the bravest Boggle of all.

The Ballad of BeWILDerwood
All the fun of the first book - but in rhyme! Lovely bold, glossy pictures and a simpler storyline bring the enchanting world of Swampy and BeWILDerwood to life for younger readers.

Come and visit

BeWILDerwood

A Curious Treehouse Adventure

A huge forest of wild family fun and outdoor adventure

Treehouses, zip wires, jungle bridges, Crocklebogs, boat trips, marsh walks and really yummy food.

"Did you know that you can come and play in BeWILDerwood yourself and run in the footsteps of Swampy and his brave friends?"

'One of the 50 most fabulous things to do in the world'